MW00387146

A DEEPER LOVE

SUBTITLE: A JOURNEY OF THE HEART

AUTHOR: DONNELL JORDAN

CITY AND STATE OF PUBLICATION: BALTIMORE, MARYLAND

(TITLE PAGE)

A DEEPER LOVE

A JOURNEY OF THE HEART

DONNELL JORDAN

CITY AND STATE OF PUBLICATION: BALTIMORE, MARYLAND

(COPYRIGHT PAGE)

A DEEPER LOVE

A JOURNEY OF THE HEART

DONNELL JORDAN

PUBLISHED BY:

ALL RIGHTS RESERVED. NO PART OF THIS BOOK MAY BE
REPRODUCED OR TRANSMITTED IN ANY FORM OR BY ANY MEANS,
ELECTRONIC OR MECHANICAL, INCLUDING PHOTOCOPYING,
RECORDING OR BY ANY INFORMATION STORAGE AND RETRIEVAL
SYSTEM, WITHOUT WRITTEN PERMISSION FROM THE AUTHOR,
EXCEPT FOR THE INCLUSION OF BRIEF QUOTATIONS IN A REVIEW.

COPYRIGHT © 2016 BY JONATHAN JORDAN

FIRST EDITION, 2016

(DEDICATION PAGE)

This story is dedicated to my confidante, my best
friend and the greatest love I have ever known (she
knows who she is); to my children who give me
strength and my closest family and friends who
encourage me to push on…

(EPIGRAPH)

I truly believe that we are creatures of our own
making, to those who insist that a divine presence
is responsible for choosing the path of the heart
and inspiring all that follows I would say nay! It
is the heart and the heart alone that knows the
truth. The idea that one could love another
without condition, forsaking all others is a
testament to the power of love itself. Much like a
ship caught in the fog of night drifting towards a
light in the distance, the heart alone knows the
way…..

TABLE OF CONTENTS

(ABOUT THE AUTHOR)

Jonathan Jordan is not a professionally trained
writer by any means, he is simply a person who
enjoys a good story about romance and love and all
that falls in between. He has also been a lover of
poetry since his early days in junior high school.
This book is not based on actual events and any
similarities to individuals or events past or
present, living or dead is not intended.

(ACKNOWLEDGEMENT)

I would like to take this opportunity to thank everyone who has every listened to and enjoyed one of my poems or short stories, everyone who has ever loved and been loved, everyone who has ever held someone's hand and spoke to them of matters of the heart. To my children who inspire me everyday, to my family who have spoken of this talent they see in me and to the one who's love for me has known no end.

History

This book has taken years to complete, begun in 2007 then cast aside in March of 2008 when my father passed away unexpectedly. Confined to a dusty closet until only recently when I felt a need to complete this work.

Many people contributed to this book, most indirectly, it is my fondest hope that you enjoy the journey I have in store for you.

THE RECEPTION

Michael approaches the podium, he pulls a single sheet of paper from the inside breast pocket of his suit and after pausing to survey the room stands frozen…eye's fixated on Lisa. After several moments of silence, he begins to speak. "I came here tonight not knowing exactly what I would say or even how to say it, what does one say to describe something that has filled me with so much love and happiness over the past ten years. I've searched my heart and after considerable thought, I have decided to share with you a poem that I wrote some time ago…I'm not much for public speaking so I hope this comes out ok." Michael begins to read from the piece of paper in his hand

Years ago, I took your hand and pledged my love for life. We walked the isle then said those words and you became my wife. Beautiful and strong you are...my backbone thru and thru. Each night before I sleep...I thank the lord above for you. Tender are your kisses, full of love your warm caress. With you I've watched my dreams come true...my life is truly blessed. Some folks believe in time love fades, "nothing lasts" they say, not true, for me you'll have my heart, until my dying day

As Michael steps from the podium, arms outstretched towards his wife Lisa, she rises to meet him. After a tender kiss, they move to the dance floor for the first dance of the night, Ronald Isley's "Real Woman" begins to play and Michael softly mouths the words "you are my kiss of life" in Lisa's right ear while they move together in what could only be described as a rhythmic flow of emotions, a tear begins to slide down Lisa's left cheek as their embrace becomes tighter. They hardly notice when the song ends, stopping only for the applause of the guests who rise to their feet to offer up a standing ovation to the couple. Michael and Lisa motion to their daughter Donielle to join them on the floor, the three embrace, then Michael leaves the two on the floor and returns to his seat. As Michael surveys the room, his eye's can't help but return to the dance floor, Lisa, the woman he has loved for what seems like forever looks as beautiful now as the day he first saw her over a decade ago……..

(FIRST DANCE)

It was Friday evening and Michael was at the lounge his
God parents owned in Northeast Baltimore. He was there
that night, just relaxing, but also helping out if
needed. Normally he would come in, have a drink, flirt a
little, dance a little, help out on restocking the bar
and watch the door. On this particular night, Michael
had just sat down in a booth across from the bar and
glanced towards the door as a small group entered. There
were two females and a male, nothing too unusual for a
Friday evening, except for the tight green suit the guy
happened to be wearing. Michael tried hard to contain
himself; that was the funniest thing he'd seen all day,
as he sipped from a glass of white wine in front of him,
Michael was suddenly drawn to one of the women who was
accompanying the guy, she was light brown skin with a
slightly thick build, well dressed in a short blue skirt
and white top, medium height, long braided hair and very
attractive.

Try as he might, he was unable to take his eyes off of her. A few moments later his sister Mary approached him at the table and whispered into his ear "she's going to think you're a stalker if you keep staring at her like that"……Michael began to smile; I was just checking out her toes, you know I love a woman with pretty feet……"it's too dark in here for you to see her feet", Mary replied.

Why don't you just go over and introduce yourself to her……any other time, you would have jumped up and met her at the door…Mary said.

"I think she's with the guy in the green suit, he's paying for her drink, don't want to break up a happy home…Michael says, he laughs then gets up and walks to the next room where the dance floor is to speak to the DJ. Ronald the DJ has been spinning records for years……he's played in most of the clubs in Baltimore and has a loyal following who would gladly patronize any club he plays at. Michael and Ronald have been friends since he dated Mary years ago. Hey man, can you put on that record by Aaron Hall I like? Michael asks? I feel like dancing.

"Ok, give me a minute," Ronald replies. Michael quickly searches for Mary and after a few minutes, they hit the dance floor, as the song "Don't Be Afraid" begins to play, Michael and Mary begin to dance, so in tuned are their steps and moves, you almost forget that they are brother and sister, every movement in sync with the tempo of the music, every sway a single motion, several other couples on the floor melt away to the side and begin to join the crowd encircling the dance floor as Michael and Mary continue on. At the conclusion of the song, you hear a round of applause from the crowd, the dance is finished and Michael returns to his seat while Mary enters the kitchen. A short time later, Michael see's the woman from earlier on the dance floor with the guy in the green suit, he approaches the second woman and asks her if her two friends are a couple, "those two" she replies; oh no we all just hang out together, what's your name? she asks, "I'm Michael" "it's nice to meet you Michael, I'm Karen, Wait right here", she gets up and goes to the dance floor, she returns a short time later with the woman and introduces her; "this is my friend Lisa, Lisa, this is Michael". Michael is speechless for a moment; "I'm sorry, I didn't mean to interrupt your dance, I mean I didn't think your girlfriend would go and get you, I just wanted to know who you were". Well now you know. My song is playing, are you going to dance with me? Lisa asks. Michael takes Lisa by her left hand and leads her to the dance floor, as they begin to move to Ronald Isley's "Real Woman" Lisa leans in and asks

Michael "do you think we'll get a standing ovation too"?
Michael laughs…that's my sister by the way, I didn't ask
who she was Lisa replies, but you too looked good dancing
together.

After the dance Michael walks Lisa back to her table, he
asks if she'll join him for a dance again before she
leaves and she replies "maybe", "maybe is better than
no"; Michael replies. He returns to his seat at the bar,
then moments later is summoned to help bring liquor up
from the basement to replenish the bar, after several
minutes, Michael is back at his seat, but now the hour is
late, as patrons begin to leave Michael approaches Lisa
for the final dance only to find that she too is about to
leave. You should have come back to me earlier; Lisa
says, you waited too long, I didn't drive tonight, so I
have to leave with my friends, do you have a number?
Yes, Michael replies, he gives Lisa his number and she
does the same, do you mind if I walk you outside, Michael
asks.

"Yeah", it's kind of chilly outside; where's your coat,
Lisa asks? I'll be ok Michael responds, I won't be
outside that long. Outside, Michael stops at the curb
and watches as they walk across the street, Lisa turns
back and shouts out "your not married are you"? Nah,
"not married" Michael replies as he turns to re-enter the

lounge.

Several days past before Michael works up the nerve to call Lisa, he's at work as a driver for a local limousine company when he decides to dial her number. The phone rings several times before the answering machine picks up, "this is Lisa…I'm not here, you know what to do"…Michael begins to smile…he hangs up the phone and doesn't leave a message. Its four p.m., Michael is picking up a client who's coming in by private plane, he's sitting out at the entrance gate to Signature Airport when his phone rings, its David, his boss; Michael, when your thru with that run can you pick up a client from the Marriott Waterfront and drop him off at Hopkins University for a meeting? What time does he need to be there? Michael asks; He said any time before 7:00 pm, David replies. Ok, I'll keep you updated on my arrival time downtown.

Michael picks up a notepad to begin writing when the phone rings, its Stephen James, the client. "Hello this is Stephen, is this Michael"? "Yes, this is Michael Mr. James are you landing now? I'm outside the front gate, they'll escort me thru once your plane begins to taxi, excellent Michael, excellent, Stephen replies. I have to be at the hotel by 5:15 pm, do you think we can make it?

17

It shouldn't be a problem; we'll be just ahead of the traffic heading north into the city this time of day. The front gate opens and Michael starts the car up, he's driving an older model Town Car, it's been his assigned vehicle since he started with the company a few years ago, it's the oldest in the fleet and Michael's managed to keep it looking pretty good, he's also been working to have his own Chevy Suburban refurbished as an un-stretched limousine. Michael is lead around to Mr. James plane as the door opens and the stairs unfold to the Gulfstream IV, it's a beautiful plane and Michael would know, he's been on a few while working high profile jobs in the past, he once worked a gig for a foreign family of eight that came in on a plane that was originally built to seat two hundred, it had been converted to a luxury jet with bedrooms, a large kitchen, conference area and a large entertainment room. Michael's experience with "persons of interest" made him invaluable to David. Client's repeatedly requested him and often made attempts to hire him away.

 Once Michael was being considered for the Director of Operations job at the company, but when David's son Edward came on board, that job soon became unavailable. It wasn't that David didn't think Michael was a good fit for the position; it was just that David wasn't sure his son would fall in line and take direction from Michael; he thought it best to leave well enough alone.   Maybe that was for the best, as Michael didn't think too much of Edwards work ethic anyway, he was always hearing stories of Edward taking cars out for reasons not work related, detailing drivers to runs for his friends then telling them they didn't have to tip the drivers, he was also known to call in at the last minute for pick-ups when he wanted to go on a date and didn't want to drive himself because he would be drinking.   David knew of course, but it was his son; was he really going to do anything about it?   Michael steps out of the car and hurries to the rear passenger side door and opens it, as Mr. James enters the car his phone rings, Michael returns to the driver's side door after loading Mr. James's luggage in the trunk and quickly enters the vehicle, once inside, Michael asks Mr. James if he's ready to proceed; I'm ready kind sir; Stephen replies, let's get the show on the road!

 Mr. James is a multi-billionaire…he owns several large companies and has properties on three continents.   His specialty is buying up failing companies and turning them around, he's a private man, seldom seen in public, he allows his executives to be the face of his organization.

He rarely travels in groups and his schedule is a tightly guarded secret, known only to a few. Michael thought it odd at first that a person of his statue would travel without some sort of entourage, but then again, sometimes the best way to avoid detection is to be discreet, the smaller the group, the less chance you'll draw attention and because Mr. James rarely gave interviews or allowed his self to be photographed, he was somewhat off the grid…so to speak. It begins to rain and Michael reduces the speed on the vehicle, he's a trained driver and leaves nothing to chance, he overhears Mr. James talking on the phone, its apparent he's talking to a woman. "I would really like to see you, I'm only here until tomorrow and not quite sure when I'll return; what time is your appointment, I can pick you up; oh, I understand, well who cares if someone see's us? I'm tired of sneaking around too, I only visit this city a few times a year, most people don't even know what I look like; what time is your massage scheduled for, we can meet in the lobby or you can come down to the car…ok…just call me when your finished, I'll try to work out something"….the conversation ends and Mr. James is silent…..do you know the Harbor Court Michael? Yes, Mr. James, are you going there, we can be at the courtyard in 20 minutes; no, no…I can't go there just yet, my lady friend is having a massage and it would be uncomfortable for us both if we were to be seen together there right now; still, maybe a

quick visit wouldn't hurt. If you don't mind me asking
Mr. James, is your friend at the hotel now? I only ask
because if she's at the Harbor Court, I could possibly
arrange a discreet meeting for you two to talk briefly,
"that……Michael, would be a very good thing, in fact that
would be a great thing" Michael picks up his cell phone
and dials a number, after a few seconds he begins to
speak, hey Jeff, need a favor, can you get me thru to the
7th floor for a few minutes, I need to arrange a quick
meet…you can, great man, I owe you one, yeah I
know…Tonya's birthday is coming up…I got you
covered…..we'll be there in fifteen minutes. So, what
did you do before this Michael…Stephen asks…..I worked in
security, some transportation, a lot of advance work.
Were you in the military? No, but I met a guy about
twenty years ago who had his own company, he was former
government, taught me everything from the ground up…I'm
taking you to the Condo's of Harbor Court Mr. James,
there's a walkway I've used a few times for some of my
clients, it's a direct route to the health club and a
little more private.

They reach the building and Michael parks in the driveway, Jeff the doorman comes out to meet them, Michael hands him the keys; we'll just be a few minutes Jeff; as they enter the building and Michael directs Mr. James to a side elevator, after a few minutes they exit on the 7th floor and walk a short distance before coming upon a glass door. Please call your friend Mr. James and ask if she can meet you over near the atrium…she'll understand. After Mr. James places the call, Michael opens the door and they exit to what appears to be a rooftop area with an outdoor tennis court and plants, Mr. James looks across the garden of flowers and sees a familiar site…thank you Michael…I'll just be a few minutes…take your time Mr. James; Michael replies.

(TELL ME EVERYTHING)

Lisa and her friend Karen are at the mall, they stop at
the food court for drinks and Lisa decides to check her
phone, you know, that guy never did call me, did you get
his number...Karen asks, I can't remember...someone called
me, but didn't leave a message, I didn't program his
number in my phone...oh well...so what store do we hit first?
I have to take these shoes back while we're here, I'm
tired of carrying them around, I also want to stop at
Macy's. "Girl...I'm not trying to be here all day, I got a
date later, it's been a while and I'm getting some
tonight; says Karen...Lisa looks up at Karen, then
smiles...you a freak girl, you know that's right..Karen
replies, "I'll be a freak tonight for sure"....they both
share a laugh as they head off in the direction of
Macy's.

Mr. James and Michael exit the Condo front entrance and walk towards the car; she's an incredible woman Michael, I've never known anyone like her….I understand Mr. James and of course I won't mention this to anyone at all, Michael replies. Michael, I asked for you specifically because I know of your reputation, you've driven for quite a few people I know, I believe you when you say you'll honor my privacy. The car pulls away from the front of the building and heads to its destination, The Hyatt, after pulling up in the driveway, Michael exits the vehicle and retrieves Mr. James's bag from the trunk, a bellman comes over with a cart and Michael places the bag on it. He then opens the rear car door and Mr. James steps out, Michael, can you pick me up tomorrow morning at 7:00 AM? I have a meeting in Hunt Valley. Sure thing Mr. James, I'll be here, Michael starts to turn away and Stephen stops him, take your lady out to dinner tonight on me Michael, he then hands Michael a $100 dollar bill, surprised; Michael starts to speak, but Stephen stops him, please have a good time tonight Michael, see you in the morning. Michael gets in the car and heads over to the next job, he calls the dispatcher; hey Cheryl, can you call the client over at the Waterfront hotel and tell him I'll be there in 10 minutes; sure thing Michael, I'll tell him you'll be in the front of the hotel, his name is Mr. Bradley, you had him before, about five months ago, he's a professor with Hopkins. Oh ok, I think I remember him. Michael reaches the hotel and pulls up across from the cab stand. He reaches for his phone and it rings….hello, this is Michael, can I help you? I don't know…can you? Lisa asks; I was going to delete your number from my phone….Lisa?...Michael is caught off guard for a moment…wow, it's nice to hear from you…I want to talk to you, but I'm working, could I please call you back? Sure you can….I'm on the way home, you can call me anytime tonight after 7:00pm….Sprint huh, Michael laughs….Lisa chuckles…yeah you know it…she laughs again, I'll talk to you later…if you remember to call. "I'll call", Michael replies before hanging up. Mr. Bradley comes out and Michael finishes the run before heading home for the evening. While driving, he starts to think about Lisa, he dials her number in hopes that she'll answer; the phone rings twice, then Lisa picks up; hello Michael, you called back…yes I did; what are you up to? I'm home now and getting ready to take a bath, oh, I apologize, didn't mean to disturb you…no its ok; Lisa replies. What do you do for a living? I drive for a limo company, mostly corporate stuff; I don't do weddings, proms or anything like that. What about you? Oh, I work in a nursing home, but I've also done some commercials. I've done maybe a dozen, for products like Pepsi, Tide, Aspirin, etc.

I even did a commercial for an online dating site, it was cheesy, but I got paid well for it. That's what I want to get back into. Wow; that's interesting; so how do you feel about the nursing thing? It's a job, I got into it a few years ago when my mom got sick and it kind of stuck, I also worked for Bank of America downtown in their operations center for a while. I thought about getting back into acting, but the last agent I worked with retired and it's been difficult finding another good one, the break has been good though, it's given me a chance to focus on something else for a change. Is your mom better…Michael asks. Yes, she had to have a kidney transplant, that took a lot out of her…and me, but we got thru it. Is your father still alive? Michael asks. No, he passed away almost eight years ago; I'm sorry to hear that, Michael responds, my dad passed away three years ago, it was only the last year or so before he passed that I really got to know him. Michael becomes silent for several seconds then speaks, so…are you single and if so, why?...Well, my last friend cheated on me, the one before him cheated on me too…so I don't really have a lot of patience right now for players….my last boyfriend was also my manager, so you can imagine how that turned out. When we broke up I actually turned down work just so I wouldn't have to give him any money (Lisa laughs), I just waited until my contract expired with him.

Do you like driving other people around all day? Well, I don't really look at it like that, Michael replies. I only work with corporate clients because there's less hassle, they usually just want to get to where they're going and they tip well. I'm working on getting my own company up and running. I'm putting my first vehicle on the road in a month or so and then I'll add a second vehicle and driver shortly afterwards……if things go as planned. Sounds like you have it all worked out…nothing like a man with a plan, Lisa chuckles….we'll see, Michael replies. Well, I have to go now, give me a call later when you have time, says Lisa…will do…Michael replies.

Its 6:25 a.m., Michael reaches the courtyard of the Hyatt hotel. He gets out, opens the passenger side rear door in anticipation of Mr. James's arrival. Suddenly the phone rings, its David asking him if he can do another run later that evening to Dulles. Michael explains that he's not quite sure what time Mr. James is leaving and doesn't want to commit to another run.

Sounds like you are in demand there Michael…Mr. James states as he's walking toward the car. No, we're just short staffed…someone booked a run without checking to make sure we had a driver available. Why doesn't your manager just do it himself? Mr. James asks? That's not likely to happen, Michael replies. He doesn't leave the office during the day unless it's absolutely necessary. What's more necessary than good customer service...Mr. James replies. I agree, sometimes you have to lead from the front, Michael replies. Mr. James nods in agreement before entering the car. After closing the door, Michael gets in and starts to pull away from the hotel, we should be there in roughly 40 minutes Mr. James, that's fine Michael, I have to go over some things before we get there anyway, don't rush.

Regret

I saw you today......but you didn't see   me,

How could I have let you go?

That smile, your walk...the way you stand

I won't sleep tonight I know!

Each time I open the closet door,

I see that shirt...the one you wore,

At night, you know...to get your way

That shirt that always made me say

Damn...I love you

Do you think of me...at night I mean......

I think of you...it's true, I do

I close my eyes and hold you tight......

If only I had treated you right,

To see you now and know that I,

Will never again lay by your side

If only I had treated you right...

If my stupid pride weren't in the way,

I would have been man enough to say,

Damn, I love you...please take me back....

(SECOND CHANCES)

Rodney Ingram is Lisa's former boyfriend and manager.
He's had a difficult time since his break up with Lisa
and spends most of his time searching for that right job
that'll make Lisa want to come back to him again. Lisa
and Rodney dated for almost 3 years. During that time,
Rodney played loose and fast with Lisa, he never really
knew how to define their relationship. Most of the time
when they were together it was just sex, he expressed to
her early on that he wasn't interested in getting married
and wasn't sure about kids. Lisa herself stated many
times that she wasn't looking for a long term thing...she
just wanted to take it slow and see what developed. It
started innocently enough...they met at a restaurant,
introduced by a mutual friend. Rodney sold her on his
ability to get things done...he knew people who knew people
and those people could get Lisa work. Lisa signed a
contract with Rodney, they started dating shortly after.
It started out fine at first, they were inseparable, they
enjoyed hanging out, Rodney stayed busy selling Lisa and
Lisa enjoyed being the center of his attention.

Rodney wasn't the most romantic guy Lisa ever dated, but then again neither was the guy before him. Lisa was an incredibly sexual woman, all she cared about at this point was having someone to kick it with on the regular…Rodney could handle that job just fine.

After about a year, things started to cool between the two, Rodney and Lisa were spending less time together, Jobs came less frequently and Lisa began wondering where Rodney was spending his time when not with her. One night while Rodney was visiting and taking a shower, Lisa heard Rodney's phone vibrating in his pants pocket, she took it out and read a message from someone named Rhonda. The message struck at Lisa like a knife…she was talking about how nice it was spending the evening with Rodney the night before and how she enjoyed the love making session, even praising his oral skills. Lisa placed the phone on the bed and sat down, not sure what to say to Rodney, she began thinking about her feelings and how she now felt betrayed by this man she thought of as her partner.

Rodney exited the bathroom and stood in front of Lisa wrapped in a towel, with a devilish grin on his face he looked at Lisa and then let the towel fall to the floor…Lisa looked up at Rodney and said "your phone buzzed while you were in the shower"……I think there's somewhere else you need to be right now….Rodney stood silent for a few minutes as Lisa looked on, then got dressed and left quietly, it took several weeks before Lisa would even agree to speak to him again, they never spoke about the text message from Rhonda. It was only during the weeks of non communication that Rodney realized how much he really loved Lisa, but now it seemed that ship had sailed…

To his frustration, Lisa hadn't shown any interest in wanting to work with him again, he's pitched fashion shows, local commercials, etc. He's been hard at work on a spot in an upcoming sitcom being shot in Vegas about two girlfriends rooming together while working in a casino on the strip. He hasn't told Lisa yet because he wants to finalize arrangements for her audition. He also wants to make sure he has a new contract in place with her first.

Rodney pulls up at the corner from Lisa's job, he can
see her standing out front, it's her break time and she
looks as though she just returned from picking up food.
Rodney stays in the car and decides to call her on her
cell phone. The phone rings, Lisa answers......hi Rodney......hey
you...Rodney replies, I need to get with you about a new
project, when can we schedule something...Rodney asks?
What kind of project...Lisa asks. It's something I've been
working on for a little while now, it's looking more and
more like it's going to happen, can we get together?
Lisa reluctantly agrees, but tells Rodney that she
doesn't want to be kept in the dark about what he's
doing. Rodney agrees and they settle on the following
Friday, they'll meet down at Melba's around 7:00 pm.
Rodney wants to have a contract put together first and
Lisa has always been more agreeable after a few drinks.
Seated in his car, Rodney can't help but think about his
past with Lisa, the time they spent together as a couple,
taking trips, watching movies...making love. Rodney has
had many relationships over the past year and a half, but
none matched the intensity of what he had with Lisa.

He often thought about that night when Lisa read the message from Rhonda......initially there was more anger than anything else...I mean, who was she to check his phone he thought to himself...how long had she been doing that and maybe he should have been checking hers as well. He's never really gotten over Lisa and to some extent he still blames her for not forcing him to define their relationship earlier on. He still keeps the pajama's she use to sleep in whenever she stayed over at his place, they haven't been washed since she last wore them, her scent vaguely apparent reminds him of a time when they were one.

(ROAD TRIP)

Michael finally arrives at the destination in Hunt
Valley, a medical research company. The place still
looks the same, he thought....I use to work here years
ago....really...Mr. James asks...what did you do here? I
worked in security...I was assigned to a division president
as his driver. I was only here about a year...I left to go
into private investigations. That's interesting
Michael...you'll have to tell me some stories sometime
about the types of cases you worked on. Michael exits
the vehicle, walks around to the passenger side and opens
the door for Mr. James...I'll be out in an hour or so
Michael...no problem Mr. James...I'll be here. Michael
closes the door and returns to the driver's seat, he's
been thinking about Lisa for most of the morning, just
wondering what she was up to...whether she was at work,
what she was wearing, etc. He reaches for his journal
which he keeps between the seat and arm rest and starts
to thumb thru the pages. A few seconds pass, then the
phone rings, hello, this is Michael. You don't have my
number programmed in your phone? Hi Lisa, I do, but I
never assume it's the person listed who's calling,

how's your day going? Its going…..I just finished with a patient….I am so tired of this job, you have no idea…I probably have some idea……Michael chuckles. I'm just ready to do something else, I'm tired of this city, tired of this life and not being able to get out and do what I want to do when I want to. If my mother was better, I would have been gone from here a long time ago. Wow…..well have you thought about doing more commercials again or trying to step it up into maybe movies or something? I've tried, been on a few casting calls, but nothing recently, just trying to get my mom squared away before I start thinking about diving back into the business again. I'm also trying to decide whether I should get a new manager first. What would be so bad about going back to your last manager, I mean, he was good at getting you jobs right? Yeah…but he comes with strings attached and besides, he was cheating on me…I can't look at him without remembering that. I did agree to meet him for drinks this week though……I think he's working on another commercial or something, we don't have a contract anymore so at least I can walk away without any confusion.

What do you really want to do…Michael asks? I'd just like to find one really good project to work on, something that would take me away from here and let me breath for once….if it wasn't for Netflix and orange soda I don't know what I would do……she laughs…when you close your eyes at night, do you only think about driving other people around…Lisa asks? Well, I think about a lot of things, I like the industry I work in and most of the people are appreciative of good service. I applied once to a larger transportation company that was international, I thought man…if I could get on with these guys, I could really do something, they were a government contractor, but hired mostly ex military people with clearances. I'm content to keep doing what I'm doing until I have enough to get the work finished on my own vehicle. What do you have that's being worked on…Lisa asks? I'm having a custom interior put in a truck I want to start using, most clients don't do stretch vehicles anymore, the clientele I'm going after wants to arrive safely and most of the time without much fanfare…I have an SUV, not stretched, just altered inside to seat four, with a small bar, lap tables and monitors. It'll be nice…when it's finally finished. Sounds good…sounds like you really got it all worked out, when I make it big and can afford you…you can come pick me up for a ride...I want a stretch though…Lisa chuckles…I'll come get you in that SUV and you'll be just as happy…I'll even have a rose in my hand…to make you feel even more special…Michael replies…they share a laugh, but then Lisa realizes she needs to return to work, I'll give you a call a little later Michael…ok, talk to you soon…Michael replies.

Mr. James comes out of the building and Michael quickly exits to get the door…all done Michael, I'm hungry, what do you recommend that's on the way back to the hotel? Well, depending on what you have a taste for, there are several options. I just want simple…nothing fancy…something local would be nice…Michael knows just where to take him. There's an Italian place I recommend that's on the way…the foods pretty good and it's a comfortable place to eat. 20 minutes later they arrive at Valentino's restaurant on Northern Pkwy. Michael finds a parking spot close to the entrance…gets out and opens the door for Mr. James…I know you have to be hungry Michael, please join me…Michael agrees.

After entering they are seated quickly and after ordering drinks, Mr. James starts up a conversation…so……tell me a little more about yourself Michael…I know you use to be a security officer, you drive a limo now…what do you have planned next for yourself? Well, I'm working on starting my own car service…I think I can put together a nice little business driving for myself until the next big thing comes along. I'm not getting any benefits right now so I wouldn't really be losing anything by going solo…I can make more on my own then what the company is paying me. I'm just trying to go slow, get in every run I can and put a little away each chance I get…I'm not far from where I want to be. Have you discussed your plans with your current employer…seems to me that they would work hard to keep you around. I have, I even considered staying, but a position I was interested in, went to someone else…it happens, you just keep rolling……no problem. Mr. James studies Michael for a moment…then turns to the menu…what's good here? Michael looks up at Mr. James…everything…try the Linguini…it's a favorite. What about you…I've read a few articles about you…you seem to have interests all over the place…oil and gas, solar energy, publishing, broadcasting…what are you NOT into?

Mr. James smiles…

Michael, there are a lot of opportunities out there for someone like you…keep your eyes open…I think when you least expect it…things will happen for you.

What about your personal life…is there a misses…Mr. James asks? Michael smiles…nah….I kind of just met someone, but not sure if there's anything there yet…just starting to get to know each other. Well Michael…take my advice…if there's even the slightest chance that she could be the one…don't let too much time pass before you tell her….trust me…you'll regret it. The food arrives…I'm famished…everything looks great Michael…dig in.

After the meal, they return to the car and Michael drives Mr. James back to the hotel…I'm going to relax for an hour or so Michael, can you swing back around 8:30 tonight…I want to be back in Atlanta by bed time…no problem Mr. James, I'll be here around 8:15…great…see you then. Michael closes the passenger door as Mr. James enters the hotel, he checks his phone for missed calls, then gets in and pulls away…headed for home.

While driving, Michael feels his phone vibrate, he looks down and see's a message from Lisa…she sent him a picture of herself drinking an orange soda…Michael smiles as he gets on the beltway….

(LAKE ROLAND)

It's a few days later and Lisa decides to give Rodney a
call about the meeting. Hey…what's up girl? I was
waiting for you to call me about the meeting…what kind of
gig is this anyway…is it shoes or clothes…do I get to
keep what I wear…you know I love clothes commercials…

This is different Lisa, I wasn't going to say anything,
but it's an audition for a sitcom…it's not set in stone
yet, but its close. Lisa pauses for a moment…a
sitcom…when…where…how much does it pay…..Rodney stops
her…it's just an audition right now Lisa…they haven't set
a date yet, but they are interested, let's not put the
cart before the horse…, we have to go slow right now,
just trust me…I'll talk to you this Friday. Lisa hangs up
and immediately it hits her….she's been waiting for this
along time….she calls Michael to share the news…after a
few rings, Michael picks up…hello…hey, guess what?
Michael laughs…what? I may have an audition for a
sitcom…that's great Michael replies, what's it about? I
don't know Lisa answers while trying to calm down……I'm
going to get more details later, but I wanted to call you
and tell you about it…damn I hope this is for real…

Anyway...what are you doing...I'm bored, come pick me
up...Lisa chuckles. Ok, what time? I was kidding...I
wasn't, Michael replies....I thought you had to work today?
I do, but I could make time if I wanted too. Ok...I know
just the place, it's nice out, so let me take you to my
chill spot, its quiet, intimate and has great light
during the day, I use to take my dog there years
ago....what kind of dog do you have Lisa asks.....I had a
collie, her name was Skip, she passed away, Michael
replies. I'm sorry to hear that.....it's ok, we had some
great times together, that's what I think about. Anyway,
it's up above Northern Parkway, near the Whole Foods
store in Mt. Washington, it's a little tricky to find,
but worth the effort....trust me. Ok, I'd like to see
it...no problem, Michael replies, how about this
evening......that's doable Lisa replies, how about an hour
from now...Michael asks...it'll be six p.m., ok...I have to
work tonight, so you'll have to drop me off at work
after...is that ok? Absolutely...what's the address? 1703
Woodbourne Rd...it's just off of Hillen Rd...just call me if
you get lost......I should be good Michael replies, see you
then.

Lisa's phone rings, its Karen……what's up girl? Nothing, I'm getting ready for work, I may have some good news soon girl….what......you finally getting some? Karen starts laughing……ha, ha, ha…no, I'm talking about work wise…Rodney may have got me a gig on a TV show…I have to wait to find out, but if its good girl……I'm gone from here……wowwww…where do you have to move? I'm not sure, but I definitely think I have to relocate, I'll let you know more as I find out, I'm going to take a ride with Michael in a few, then I have to get to work, can I call you tomorrow?

Sure girl…don't forget…I want to hear more about this job thing.

Lisa goes to her room to put on her uniform, the phone rings, she looks down and its Michael……I'm coming out now…..no rush…Michael replies……take your time.

Michael's sitting at the edge of the block looking forward, scanning the doorways……this is the first time he's seen Lisa since the night they first met. Michael's wondering if she'll still look as good as she did then and more importantly, what she'll think of him…..

Lisa exits her house, she's wearing a blue sweater and what looks like a nurse's uniform......she's incredible......her braids are pulled back in a pony tail and she's not wearing makeup......she has a natural beauty and Michael can't take his eyes off her......

Beep…beep......several cars have pulled up behind Michael who's double parked, Michael pulls forward and to the curb to get out of the way of traffic. He quickly pulls down the driver's side visor to check his face in the mirror. He checks his breath, than pop's a mint before getting out of the car to open the passenger side door for Lisa.

Hey…it won't take long to get there Michael say's, I'll have you at work in no time. That's good, thanks for doing this…you didn't have to work today......yeah, but my client is tied up for a few hours, I'm good.

Michael closes the door and hurries to the driver's side to get in, as he rounds the car, the driver's side door opens, Michael gets in with a smile so wide Lisa can't help but notice…..what…say's Lisa…

You just racked up major cool points…Michael replies…

For getting in your car…no, for opening my door…small things count with me…more than you'll ever know. I'll remember that…Lisa replies.

As Michael is driving, he glances over and notices that Lisa is wearing clogs on her feet with no socks, at that moment Lisa lifts her left leg to remove the shoe from her foot, she's putting socks on and as Michael catches a glimpse of her foot, he can't help but notice how sexy it is…

Nice feet, size six?……my feet are not nice, feet are not nice! Their ugly…….what you got a foot fetish?

I don't know if it's a fetish or not, but I like to see a woman with her feet taken care of……well, as long as their clean, that's enough for me. I get a pedicure when its time and that's it…Lisa replies with a grin.

We're coming up on the park now, just three more lights……how do you know about this place?…Lisa asks. I've been coming here for over ten years, It's a beautiful park and it's never crowded…you'll love it.

As they turn on to the access road Michael slows the car……they travel along a path lined with trees on both sides……Michael lowers the front windows halfway then looks over at Lisa…take a moment to listen…

Listen to what? Lisa asks…

Wait a moment…just listen……

Ok….

Within seconds, they begin to hear the sound of running water, but there's still the sight of only trees. Eventually they come to an intersection and Michael motions to Lisa to look to her left…

That's beautiful……

I know…the first time I saw this waterfall I couldn't speak, I know it sounds corny, but its peaceful…sometimes I come out here to write or just spend some time with myself…

As they near the end of the road, Lisa sees a picnic area up ahead and notices people walking down a path with fishing poles in hand…

My father loved to fish, he use to take me with him when I was little, we would catch such big fish...

Lisa doesn't speak for a few minutes, she just stares out over the water......Michael looks at Lisa, but also doesn't speak, he senses that she's thinking about her father, Michael moves the car forward and into a parking space....

Ok, we'll get out here and walk back down, it's a short walk to the other side...there aren't any snakes out here are there?...Lisa asks.

Yes, but it's ok, I promise...they won't bother you if you don't bother them...Michael laughs...

As they head back down the road Michael takes Lisa's hand......just as he did the night they first met and begins to lead her towards the foot path.

That's a funny looking building...Lisa says. I'm not sure what that is, it's been closed since I've been coming here...I sometimes fish from the balcony attached to it. What kind of fish do you catch here? Lisa asks...

I've seen different kinds of fish come out of here...Catfish, Blues, some others I don't know what you would call......look up on top of the hill to your right...you see those houses?

Yeah, I like that one...it looks like a log cabin...just bigger...Lisa squeezes Michael's hand a little tighter as she walks on......Michael begins to speak...if you walk around the lake you'll see a lot of large homes, I don't think I could live up here surrounded by all these trees though...

As they walk further, they cross the foot bridge, Lisa glances over at the waterfall, Michael notices that Lisa is squeezing his hand a little tighter now...he doesn't speak, he just continues walking. They come to a hilltop where they see a large tree shading a bench...Michael leads Lisa over to the bench, pulls a handkerchief from his back pocket and places it flat...here, sit on this, sometimes these benches are a little sticky...

Thank you...Lisa replies...

So...tell me about this poetry you write...

Well...I've been writing now since junior high school, it's just something I like to do...

What do you write about? What do you use for inspiration?

Different things, most of my poems are inspired by the people I meet, things I see or hear….

Do I inspire you...Lisa asks?

Maybe, but if I was going to write something about you…I wouldn't tell you…

Why not?

No reason…I just wouldn't…

Recite one for me now? Lisa asks…

You serious…

Yeah…let me hear something…

Ok…let me think for a minute…Michael closes his eyes…takes a breath, then opens his eye's, looks directly at Lisa and begins to speak…

I call this one……

"Untitled"

Skin-tone of shade...so soft...so flawless

Sensual..........................you are

Statuesque......so full of grace

Elegant...........................you are

So strong...so spirited...unlike no other

Confident...........................you are

With eye's so bright...so wide...inviting

Beautiful...........................you are

But what of feelings, that lay beneath?

What secrets would your heart reveal....

If given voice to speak...

Tell me of your wants and dreams

What drives your spirit?

What brings you peace?

What comforts you at night?

For me it is the thought of you...

My true soul mate.........you are!

Lisa is speechless…she wonders for a moment who the poem was written for…

I like that…have you ever thought of having your poems published?

I have, but I'm working on this limo thing right now….that's my priority…

After sitting for a while and looking out over the water, Michael glances down at his watch….oh shit! We gotta go…..he grabs Lisa's hand and heads back to the foot path. We should be able to make it downtown in about 25 minutes, Lisa hurries behind him still smiling. In the car, Michael turns on the radio and begins searching stations, do you have any CD's…Lisa asks, of course…check the glove compartment. Lisa opens the glove box in front of her and finds an assortment of different artists, she settles on a CD by Najee, after putting it in, she reclines the seat back and closes her eyes.

Michael glances over at her as a warm feeling begins to take hold, as he looks over at her again and again…taking in the sight of Lisa quietly enjoying the music, Michael silently whisper's…"beautiful"…..

Michael eventually makes it to Lisa's job, after opening the door to let her out, Lisa gives Michael a peck on the right cheek,…thank you Michael, I needed that more than you know…..Michael smiles, no problem darling…I'll give you a call.

Later, Lisa's standing at the nurse's station, who was that good looking dude who dropped you off....Lisa turns, its Becky, her supervisor, oh, that's Michael, he's just a friend…a friend huh…….single?...Becky asks? Lisa glances over at Becky…yeah….why?

Just asking girl…you two just friends right? Yeah…just friends, Lisa chuckles as she turns to walk away….

The next night, Lisa gets a phone call from Michael, hey you…..you busy? No, just rolling my hair…what are you doing…Lisa asks? Pulling up to McDonalds, just finished an airport run, I've been thinking about McDonalds fries all day…Michael replies…..you and me both, Lisa chuckles. I wanted some earlier, but didn't have any money on me, I hate getting paid twice a month, I just cashed my check and It's gone already…let me grab you something while I'm here…Michael asks…it's ok, I'll be alright, Lisa replies…no, it's no big deal, what do you want? Well….since your there…Lisa laughs, just grab me some fries and an orange soda. Got it, be there shortly…later, Michael calls Lisa back, I'm out front….Lisa comes out and runs up to the driver's side window, she's wearing silk pajama bottoms and a white tank top with slippers…Michael can't resist staring at her breast…here you go…thanks babe, Lisa smiles…call me tomorrow…I will, Michael replies, before driving away.

  Lisa is back in her room, as she lifts the fries from the bag, she sees a receipt and what looks like forty five dollars at the bottom of the bag, she calls Michael to tell him he forgot his change,…after a few rings, Michael answers the phone, hey babe…you forgot your change…oh, well, I'm not turning around I can tell you that…Michael smirks…just keep it, I'm good, I promise…you can treat me to fries the next time…Lisa pauses before responding ok. After the call, she lay's across the bed, she looks at the receipt and realizes Michael didn't get anything for him self, he brought her fries and soda, then left the change of a $50.00 dollar bill for her.

The next morning Michael is at the car wash, he gets a call from David……Michael, can you do a run for me this

afternoon? I think so, Michael replies, who and where?
It's an old client of ours in town for the day…he's
staying at the Hilton downtown…he has a few meetings…then
will be returning to the hotel. Ok, I'll take care of
it…have Cheryl send me the info. Michael finishes up
then heads home to prepare.

(JUST BREATHE)

It's Friday evening and Lisa's getting dressed to go meet
Rodney when the phone rings……hello? Hey Lisa, it's me.
Hey…I was just getting dressed…are we still on? Well,
that's why I called, I had something come up, I can't
make it tonight, but want to come by tomorrow
afternoon…is that cool? Rodney…what's going on…you asked
to meet me, now your canceling…tell me what's going
on…Lisa demands…its no big deal, I just had something
come up…I'll see you tomorrow…ok? Ok…Lisa replies before
hanging up. She sits down on the bed speechless….shaking
her head…she picks up the remote before turning off the
lights and lying back on the bed.

Lisa's just starting to get settled when she hears her
mother's voice calling out her name…Lisa…Lisa…I can't
hardly breath……Lisa rushes into her mother's room and
immediately checks her pressure, did you take your pills
today mama…Lisa asks? I don't remember…her mother
replies…Lisa runs into the bathroom to get some water,
she grabs her phone from her nightstand and after
returning to her mother's room and giving her a cup of
water, she calls 911. They should be here soon mama…it'll
be ok….I don't need to go to no hospital babe…I'm just a
little winded….her mother says….let's just wait and see
what the paramedics say, ok mama? Lisa rushes into her
bedroom to put on some sweat pants and a shirt. Soon the
paramedics arrive and after checking her mother's
pressure they decide to take her to the hospital as a
precaution.

Lisa's in the ambulance, her head is spinning, she's watching the EMT's stabilize her mother for the trip to the hospital, she's seen this a hundred times with patients at the center where she works, but this is her mom...suddenly she sinks back in the seat...Michael comes to mind, she pulls out her phone and dials his number, after several rings, he answers...Lisa? What's wrong? It's my mother, their taking her to the hospital...I don't know why I called...I'm sorry...I'm sorry I woke you....Michael quickly asks, which hospital are you going to? I don't know...I think Union Memorial...we're leaving now, I'll call you back. The ambulance pulls away...Michael is left sitting on the bed holding his phone.

It's a few hours later at the hospital…Lisa's sitting in the room with her mom who's now asleep. Lisa's looking down at her…she loves her, but sadly begins to realize that she's not going anywhere…her mother is going to need care, she'll need someone at the house with her. Lisa's been waiting a long time for something to happen, finally there's a chance for her to make a break…live her life the way she always intended and she can't go….a sense of dread washes over her, suddenly the walls begin to close in, she needs to get out, take a walk, catch her breath…she takes off thru the door and out down the hallway…she's looking for the lobby, but can't seem to remember how to get there…was it left or right?...it all looks the same, suddenly as she feels the tears begin to build up and almost explode…she reaches the double doors leading to the lobby and exit…she pushes the door release and walks thru the doors, she scans the room for the exit and there off to the side she sees something that stops her in her tracks…

Michael is sitting in the lobby, he's leaning back as if he's been there a while, he's wearing headphones, his eye's are closed. Lisa pauses taking a breath, then walks over to sit down beside him…she places a hand on his leg, he opens his eye's…how's your mom? She's resting, that's good…that's good……Michael replies. Lisa lays her head on Michaels shoulder, Michael reaches down into a bag on the floor in front of him and retrieves an orange soda…here…I thought you could use this…Lisa takes the bottle…holding it tightly she moves closer to Michael before closing her eyes…

Sometime later a doctor wakes Lisa…hi, I'm Doctor Evans…your mother's doing better, we're going to keep her for a little while longer just to make sure she's ok…you go home and we'll call you when's she's ready to leave. Michael stands up…come on Lisa, I'll take you home…can I go with you...Lisa asks? I don't want to be home alone…yeah…its cool, I have an extra bedroom…just don't talk about my dirty dishes in the sink…Lisa chuckles…ok, if you don't talk about my snoring…they leave the hospital and walk out to the car.

As Michael is driving, he looks over at Lisa who is leaning back with her eyes closed…she opens her eyes and Michael quickly looks back towards the road…why are you single again…Lisa asks?

It's complicated…I'm ok though….your not an axe murderer or anything crazy like that…are you? I'm not going to find somebody tied up under the bed or anything am I?…Lisa laughs…nah….your safe…….Lisa settles back in the seat and closes her eyes again, Michael's eye's turn towards Lisa once more before returning to the road.

They arrive at Michael's apartment building in northeast Baltimore, after parking Michael nudges Lisa…hey you…..we're here. Lisa slowly opens her eyes…where are we? We're over near Frankford, not far from your house. Michael helps Lisa out of the car and they walk across the parking lot to his building. Once there, it's just 2 floors up to his apartment. They get inside and Lisa sits down and Michael heads for the bathroom. Michael lays out an extra face cloth and towel for Lisa then goes into the bedroom and grabs a t-shirt and pair of sweatpants for Lisa then returns to the front room.

Lisa's looking around the front room, scanning for pictures and other items associated with another female. You have a nice place, Lisa says. Thank you, I've been here now for about 7 years, I've actually outgrown the place. I laid out some things for you in the bathroom if you want to freshen up before lying down. You can have my bedroom and I'll take the second room. Lisa gets up and slowly begins to walk down the hall towards the bathroom, she scans the wall and comes across a picture of the park and waterfall Michael took her too. After pausing for a moment, she turns and looks at Michael…thank you. No problem Michael replies. Get some rest…I'll see you in the morning.

As Michael begins to clear away dishes from the sink,
he can hear rain begin to beat against his balcony
doors….he walks over and opens the blinds, pausing for a
moment, he watches the rain come down before settling in
on the couch. The rain begins to pick up and suddenly a
flash of lightning is accompanied by the crack of
thunder…Michael stares out into the night sky…listening
to the almost rhythmic beat of the rain drops as they
fall. After several minutes the rain begins to slow,
then eventually stops….

Michael looks up and can see the moon, surrounded by the
stars in a clear sky…it's the second most beautiful sight
he's seen tonight…..

While You Slept

Alone I sit, through the window I gaze, its dark...yet dimly lit,

The days been long and I am tired...still...for your touch I yearn...

I rise to my feet and approach the door...on the other side you lay...

I pause for a second...to prepare myself...for all day have I desired only this...

I turn the knob and open the door...then stand in awe and silence...

As the light of the moon reflecting off the window pane gently caresses your silhouette...

My entire life...never have I known anything as beautiful...

I move to the foot of the bed and watch as you lay...legs apart...clothed only in the shirt I gave you just hours before...

As you lay there...no false nails, no hair extensions, no make up, just you...

In all your heavenly splendor...I wondered aloud...why you chose me...

I slowly undress, then move to your side...careful not to disturb your sleep...

I have loved you since the moment I first saw you and in pleasing you I have found fulfillment

As I watch the flame from the candle that burns in the corner of the room...

I ask myself...what better way to show my appreciation, then a long kiss *goodnight...*

I rise and descend to the foot of the bed...never once taking my eye's off you...

I wonder if you've ever noticed the way I stare at your feet when you wear shoes that show off your toes...so soft...so well manicured...from here is where it begins....

The instep of your right foot...sensuous...fragrant with the scent of a body spray used earlier...

As I gently move upwards, I inhale a mixture of the spray and your essence, while hovering just inches from your body...

At your thigh, I pause and all at once...I feel the need to touch you...just a little...

I am knelt between your legs...manhood erect...heart pounding...like the conqueror who has come to claim his prize...my eagerness to act is overwhelming...yet I restrain myself...for it is in this way that mistakes are made...

The time is now...while bowed before you...deeply I inhale...then slowly with lips gently parted...I blow...your right knee...the spot I've chosen...

I hear a sigh...your head gently turns...do you feel me?

If so...don't respond...lay as you were..........

For this is only the beginning....

Michael settles in on the couch, he fluffs the pillow under his head, then closes his eyes and drifts off to sleep.

Its 7:00 am, Michael is awaken by the sound of movement in the kitchen, he opens his eye's and catches a glimpse of Lisa apparently washing dishes, she's wearing his t-shirt and a pair of his boxer shorts…he smiles as he offers a morning greeting…good morning….

Lisa looks over at Michael…I was going to fix you something real quick, but the hospital called, my mom's going to be discharged this morning…that's great, I'll take you to get her and drop you both home, Michael replies…

You don't have to do that, I know you have to work Lisa answers…it's ok Lisa…I don't have a run for a few hours…let me do this for you…it's no problem.

Shortly afterwards they arrive at the hospital and Michael finds a parking spot near the main entrance. Lisa looks over at Michael…I'll be just a minute. Lisa gets out and heads inside. As Michael sits, he can't stop thinking about Lisa and his feelings for her, he thought about how nice it would have been to wake up beside her instead of down the hall from her….several times last night, he wanted to take that walk down the hall, but stayed put. This was becoming more than he bargained for or expected….he was confused about what he should say or even if he should say anything at all.

 Lisa exits the hotel pushing her mom in a wheel chair, he can hear her mom fussing about not being allowed to walk out on her own, Lisa tries to calm her down. Michael gets out and walks to the passenger side door to open it…what's this…Lisa's mom asks, who are you? That's Michael mom, he's taking us to the house, be nice…Lisa exclaims……I'm always nice, her mom replies, Hello…Michael says…how are you this morning? I'm feeling a lot better thank you…are you dating my daughter…she don't tell me nothing. No ma'am, we're just friends…her mom looks up at Michael as he's helping her in the car…this is a nice car…thank you Michael replies. Lisa gets in and immediately puts the radio on her favorite station. Michael gets behind the wheel and looks over at Lisa…do you need to stop off anyplace on the way? No, we're good…we can just go to my house. Michael begins to pull away, oh shit…I left your sweater in the room…Lisa says to her mom…..Michael, can you wait one minute? Sure…no problem he replies, take your time. Lisa exits the car and returns inside the hospital.

You really like her…don't you? Lisa's mom asks, Michael looks at Lisa's mom and all at once his face is flush…..she is a nice person. She's not going to be here forever, you better give her a reason to stay or she'll be gone…… Michael smiles as he looks away…we're just friends……ok, if you say so…her mom replies with a grin.

Lisa returns to the car, Michael pulls away. A short time later, they reach Lisa's house. Michael helps Lisa's mom out of the car and up the steps to the front door, I got her now…Lisa says, Lisa's mom looks back at Michael, Thank You babe…Michael nods with a smile, I'll call you later Lisa, nice meeting you ma'am. Michael gets back in the car and pulls away.

(PHILLY BOUND)

Lisa's walking thru the mall with Karen, they stop in
front of Victoria Secret's, girl I need some bra's, Karen
says. Lisa laugh's, I haven't bought bra's in a while,
you need to get a man girl, then you'd have a
reason...Karen smirks...

The phone rings…Lisa answers, its Rodney, hey, can you
meet me later? Why…Lisa responds. I have some papers
for you to sign…what papers Rodney….Lisa replies. It's
just a contract, we got the audition date, I need this
signed before we go or I can't represent you. Lisa
pauses for a moment…do we need a contract…yes Lisa…we
do…I did my part, it's your turn now…I need this signed.
Lisa relents, ok…come by the house around 7:00
pm…why…don't we meet out for a drink...just come by the
house Rodney…Ok, I'll see you then. Lisa turns and looks
at Karen, you heard right....yeah, I heard, are you
excited? Yes and no, I just realized, I have to make
sure my mom is ok before I can go anywhere.

Michael is cleaning his car when the phone rings…its Mr. James…hello sir! Michael answers, hello Mike…I'm coming for a few days…more like a week, can you clear your schedule, I need you. I got you Mr. James, have you booked already or do you need me to call. Yes, Sarah booked my room, but I think she reserved one night, could you follow up on that for me if it's not too much trouble?

No problem Mr. James, I'll call now….great, my plane should be in by 7:00 pm, I'll see you then.

Its 6:15 pm, Michael arrives at the gate to Signature Flight Support. The attendant immediately recognizes him and motions for him to move forward. After a brief delay Michael is led out to the runway where Mr. James plane is expected to land in a few minutes. As he comes to a stop, he hears a familiar tune on the radio, he's listening to 95.9…Ronald Isley's……Real Woman begins to play……he's briefly transported back in time to that night when he first met Lisa…he begins to think of the dance they shared and of how much he really cares about her…he glances up to see a small plane beginning to come into view…its Mr. James plane…as he sits back and takes note of the beautiful Gulfstream…it seems to just glide towards the runway. Michaels been on a few private jets, he's even been on some much larger commercial jets converted for use by members of several Middle Eastern royal families. The Gulfstream has always been a favorite. Michael exits the car as the door opens on the plane. Michael opens his trunk then turns to see a beautiful woman walking down the stairs of the plane. She appears to be Asian, tall with short dark cropped hair and wearing a waist length tan leather coat. Michael is almost speechless…Mr. James exits seconds behind, but it's the woman Michael can't take his eyes off of. As they both approach the car Michael quickly recovers his senses…

Good evening Mr. James…did you have a good flight?...Yes I did Michael…Mr. James smiles…yes I did…let me introduce you to my assistant Tamiko……Tamiko this is Michael…I've heard a lot about you Michael…it's a pleasure to meet you ma'am…please Michael…just call me Tamiko…after all…your practically a part of our family. Michael loads the luggage then, after ensuring everyone is settled in pulls away from the tarmac.

Mr. James turns to Michael, so…I'm looking into a transportation company, I wanted to pick your brain…Ok, Mr. James, first what kind of transportation service…product or people? It's people, cars, buses, helicopters, etc…Mr. James replies. The owners run into some financial trouble, he needs a lifeline, but I'm not sure the business is salvageable.

Well, we can take a look…it could be good, what city is it in…is this a national company? It's in Philly, but it could go national under the right circumstances….

Philly's a good city for transport companies…its got a lot of corporations based there, its close to Delaware, New York and New Jersey are within easy driving distance and its not far from here and DC….it could be a nice investment. Would you be willing to go up with me, take a look and tell me what you think……off the record of course, Mr. James asks….Michael glances over at Mr. James, sure, whatever you need Mr. James.

Its 8:00 am, Michael arrives at the hotel to pick up Mr. James, they are heading to Philly to take a look at the transportation company. Mr. James exits the hotel and motions for Michael to remain in the car, he opens the door and sits up front with Michael…it's a long drive Michael, I'm just one of the guys during this drive…ok? Michael nods yes. How was your evening Mr. James? It was fine Michael, room service was a little off their game last night, I ordered a steak, it took them 2 tries to get it right. You should have had the chicken strips and fries, it's hard to screw that up and its good finger food…Michael laughs. You may have something there Michael, Stephen says before letting out a chuckle.

A couple of hours later they arrive at the offices of City Lights Limo Service, it's a big warehouse building close to the waterfront across from the Coast Guard station on Columbus Blvd. After exiting the car and entering, they find a large assortment of vehicles inside…town cars, mini-vans, suv's, stretch limousines and even a few tour buses. Did you see the heliport on Columbus as we drove up?...Stephen asks…yes, that's pretty good…what exactly is the issue here?...Michael asks. I think the owner really just wants to get out of the business…his kids don't want anything to do with it, he's tired…I think that's it… any liabilities?...No, actually, the books look good, it's a money maker, most of the staff are committed, the building is paid for. Just then, they are greeted by Richard Whitlock, he's owned the business for the past twelve years…hello, hello…how are you Stephen?

Hello Richard, I'm good…this is Michael…my good friend…after several more minutes of conversation they take a tour of the rest of the building…afterwards, Richard asks Stephen to join him in his office for a few minutes, Michael is looking over a tour bus when the phone rings...this is Michael…hey you…what's up?..it's Lisa on the other end…hey mister…how've you been? I'm good, I was just thinking of you and wanted to be nosey…I'm in Philly with a client, Michael answers…I'm sitting on a tour bus…you would love this thing...Michael chuckles…oh yeah…take a few pictures…Lisa replies…you got it. Are you all set for your big trip?...yeah, I got most of what I need to do done, I'm taking a leave of absence from work and I arranged for my cousin to look in on my mom…I just got to hustle to get the rest of this money…I still have time though. How much do you need?...Michaels asks..all of it…Lisa replies with a sigh…its cool, whatever's meant to be will be, she exclaims. It'll be ok Michael replies…you'll be ok…yeah…we'll see Lisa answers.

Michael finishes the call, promising to get back to Lisa later as Mr. James concludes his meeting with Richard. I'll be in touch soon Richard, Mr. James exclaims as he motions for Michael to prepare to leave. They board the car and head back to Baltimore.

(WINGS OUTSTRETCHED)

Michael arrives at the shop to pick up his truck, he's
hardly slept, thinking about the truck and what comes
next, no one's here yet, Michael's picked up a sandwich
from McDonalds, he begins to unwrap it when Alonzo pulls
up. Hey Mike, couldn't wait to see her huh? Michael
laughs, yeah bro, I'm ready.......Michael's upgraded a 2005
Chevy Suburban with a privacy screen, reversed seating
and a flat screen TV. It's all black and has a mini wet
bar with champagne bucket and satellite reception.
Michael had a new paint job done and new tires put on it
so it would be ready for the road. He also had it tuned
up. Alonzo pushes the button and the roll up door begins
to move, Michael is speechless as the door rises and he
begins to see the silhouette of his new truck...what I tell
you bro...did I hook you up or what? You did a great job
man, its show room man...showroom! Michael opens the door
and gets behind the wheel. The phone rings as Lisa is
getting off of work, she looks down and its Michael...guess
where I am...Michael asks? At McDonalds getting me fries
and an Orange Soda Lisa replies with a chuckle...next time
babe...I'm sitting in my truck...its finally finished! It's
tight! You'd love it. That's great babe...you should
bring it by so I can see it. I will...what are you up to?

I'm just leaving work, these swing shifts are killing
me...Lisa exclaims. So you got your truck now...when are you
quitting that other company? Soon...I just have a few
things to put in place first then I'm out the door. What
are you doing later? Do you want to get together and grab
something to eat? I'll call you later after I get
settled you can stop by the house, Lisa replies.
Ok...cool, talk to you then. Later, Lisa is sitting on the
couch thinking about Michael and all at once, she begins
to reminisce about the first time she met him. She
closes her eye's and can remember how he held her the
first time they danced, she remembers the way he smelled

as she laid her head on his shoulder, the way they both moved…as if they had known each other for ever…then she caught herself…this was Michael, the man who had become her best friend, he looked at her as a friend and nothing more. Lisa settled back on the couch and began surfing channels on the television, but her thoughts kept drifting back to Michael.

Michael stops by the office to drop off his expense reports, David looks up and see's him…hey Michael, can you give me a moment? I need to talk to you…sure…Michael replies, I'll be right there. Michael hands Delores his receipts and form, then walks into David's office. Have a seat Michael, how are you today?

I'm fine, what's up?

Michael, I need to ask you something…I want to move you into the position of Operations Manager, I know you are looking for more money and I think this might be the right time to bring you up. I'm going to be stepping back somewhat from day to day matters and with my son becoming C.O.O, I need a good person to help him shoulder the weight…so to speak. Michael looks over at David and knows exactly what's going on, he means he needs Michael to keep things straight, but his son will be in charge.

Can I take a day to think about it David? Sure Michael, I also have some paperwork for you to look at, there's an offer letter and a non-compete agreement I'll need you to sign. Its all standard, take it with you and bring it back to me.

Rodney and Lisa are going over the particulars for their trip…they'll be in Vegas for approximately four weeks and have to cover their own lodging and incidentals while there…the studio is only providing roundtrip airfare.

I think we should stay together in the same room to keep costs down, we can get a double of course, but we don't need two rooms…..Lisa looks up at Rodney, same room huh……yes, same room…look, this is business Lisa, we need to be close to the casting location and the hotels in that area are not that cheap. We get in, you nail the audition, I handle the paperwork and we're out! We can put up with each other for a couple of weeks right? Lisa's not too sure, but she really wants this…Ok, how much do you think we'll need altogether? We'll need at least $3500.00 each. That's a lot right now Rodney…I know Lisa, but we need to be there for at least three weeks, you have two separate auditions, then you have to shoot a teaser so they can see you on film. It could be another week before they decide and we need to be in town in case they need to see you while deciding. It's better to get as much done while we're there the first time.

Lisa knows he's right, I don't know where I'm going to get the money, but…I'll get it…we still have a month, lets just work at it, we'll get it done.

A few days later, Lisa and her mother are seated at the table in the kitchen....you know your cousin Nicky is coming to stay with us for a while next month. Nicky? Why is that mom..is she ok? That man of hers messed up again…she needed a change and since we got that extra bedroom, I just told her to come on down and stay here….besides…with you leaving…I can't stay here by myself, her mother says with a sly smile…Lisa looks over at her mother…you know about the trip momma? I know little girl….go on and make your plans…you'll have the money for the trip. Lisa gets up from the table and heads over to give her mother a hug…I love you momma…I know baby…I know. Later that evening, Lisa's laying across the bed, trying to figure out a way to break the news to Michael…its not like he'll really raise a fuss or anything she says…after all, he's focused on his business right now…he probably won't even notice that she's gone. She dials his number and after a few rings, Michael picks up the phone…hey you! Michael exclaims….what are you up to? Nothing much…just getting ready for bed…what are you doing…Lisa asks? I'm just sitting at my desk going over some jobs I have scheduled for tomorrow…nothing much. After a pause…Lisa just lets it out…Michael, remember the gig I told you about…well I'm leaving soon, I have the money I need and its time…I wanted to hang out with you before I leave, but I know your probably going to be busy the next week or so. Michael takes a breath…darling…I'm always busy...then after a few seconds, he begins to speak again…I'm really happy for you, I know this is something you've wanted for a long time and I hope it works out great for you. If you get a chance, we'll get together for a drink before you leave, but right now I have to finish this up…I'll hit you later…ok? Lisa pauses for a second then replies ok…before hanging up…she knew that Michael sometimes could be all business, but she wasn't quite expecting the conversation to end the way it did.

Michael's still seated at his desk, he puts down the phone, leans forward to turn off the desk lamp and then remains seated for a few minutes…he's thinking now about all the things he wanted to say to Lisa…but didn't. Michael gets up from the desk and walks over to the balcony doors and looks out into the night sky….its quite now…so much quieter than normal now…

Michael begins to get settled in for the night when the phone rings…its Stephen James…Hey Michael…hey Mr. James Michael responds…I'm going to be in Philadelphia at the end of the month, can you come up to get me? Sure thing Mr. James, where will you be? I'll be at the Limo company, Tamiko will send you the details, see you soon Michael…I hope you've been well. See you soon Mr. James.

(THE NEXT CHAPTER)

Lisa and Rodney return to their hotel after the first day at the auditions. Lisa is very tired and to be honest missing her mother and to some extent talking to Michael. You killed it today babe, Rodney exclaims…just keep that same energy going and we got it in the bag. I hope so…I didn't come all the way here to be sent back home.

I want to call my mother, but don't want to jinx it you know…I know babe, Rodney replies. We still have a few more auditions to get thru and the test shoot. Let's just go slow and get through them and see what happens…ok…Lisa replies. I don't know about you, but I could use a drink…let's go out later this evening…Lisa exclaims. Rodney cracks a smile as he loosens his tie, I could go for that…I think we earned a night out…I know you did at least, Rodney laughs as he starts to unbutton his shirt. Lisa looks over…it's been a long time since she's been out, also Rodney was starting to look pretty good sitting on that couch, Lisa didn't want to get caught up, but could easily imagine herself rolling around on that couch with him if they stayed in right now.

Lisa heads to the closet…can you run the shower for me? Sure thing, Rodney replies as he heads towards the bathroom. A few minutes later Lisa can hear the sound of water running…she grabs some underclothes and her robe then heads into the bathroom. She pauses at the mirror and then turns to see Rodney staring at her…you really are a beautiful woman Lisa……he says. Lisa walks over to Rodney and without speaking…kisses him on the lips, then steps back and slowly closes the bathroom door…Rodney stands speechless for a moment then walks over to the closet to select an outfit to put on.

It's weeks later and Michael is heading up to Philly to pick up Mr. James, he arrives at the location of the Limousine Company and notices contractors working on the property making improvements. He walks thru the front door and is directed to the upstairs offices where he notices more work going on. As he passes a corner office, he hears Mr. James call out to him...Michael, come over here. He heads towards a corner office and after passing a man working on the glass door sees Mr. James seated behind a large desk. This is a nice office Mr. James...so you decided to close the deal? That's right Michael and I got it for a song...Mr. James stands and comes from behind the desk...walking towards Michael he places his arm around Michael's shoulder and starts to walk towards the door. Michael...I want you to work for me...would you consider it? Michael stops in his tracks and looks directly into Mr. James eye's then walks towards the window offering a view of the many vehicles parked below...you know Mr. James...I would gladly work for you....which one of these is my new ride Michael asks....

Right here Michael...Mr. James answers as he walks over and places his hands on the chair behind the desk. I want you to run this company as my partner...you're the best man for the job and I won't take no for an answer! Michael feels his eyes begin to water and turns away from Mr. James just as the contractor finishes the door to the office, as he steps away Michaels name and the title of Vice President can be seen on the door. Michael immediately thinks of Lisa...

Lisa is going over her lines for the start of the test shoot, this time she'll be reading with Debra…a person also auditioning for the same part, they'll be playing opposite each other for the next hour or so. Her mind is a thousand miles away…she's having trouble remembering her cues…the argument last night didn't help things either. Debra walks over to Lisa…are you ok? Do you want to take a short break first before we start…no, I'll be ok, I just didn't get a lot of sleep last night…I'm good……Debra looks at Lisa……Ok…I know we just met, but if you need to talk….I'm available…Lisa looks over at Rodney then turns back to Debra…I'm good…Rodney stands off to the side watching, he's not quite sure if he should go over to Lisa or just give her space, Rhonda's been blowing his phone up since he left, he hasn't spoken to her but knows he'll have to deal with her eventually if he wants this thing with Lisa to work. He decides to err on the side of caution and remain where he is…we just need to get thru today and we're good…he says to himself, she'll be ok, she wants this just as much as I do…we need this…It'll be ok….I'll fix everything when we get home. Later back at the hotel, Rodney checks his phone while Lisa is in the shower and sees a text from Rhonda that almost floors him…she's pregnant and has every intention of keeping the baby. Rodney taps on the bathroom door and when Lisa responds he tells her he is going out to the store and will be right back. Rodney heads out the front door of the hotel and immediately calls Rhonda…after a few rings she answers…hello Rodney….I've been trying to reach you for a while now…why haven't you answered my calls…why did it take me to text that I was pregnant before you responded? Rodney took a breath…then spoke…please tell me you were just kidding about being pregnant. I'm keeping it Rodney…we'll talk when you get back to town. The phone goes silent on the other end as Rodney continues walking down the street towards the convenience store in silence.

The next morning as Rodney and Lisa are getting dressed to head down for a reading, Rodney's phone rings, it's the casting agent for the show, Rodney walks out onto the balcony and after a few minutes returns to the room. He sits down on the edge of the bed and after a few seconds looks at Lisa and tells her that the studio decided to cast someone else in the part. Lisa is devastated, she drops her hair brush on the floor and immediately begins to sob…is there anything we can do…she asks…no babe, they just didn't feel you were right for the part…we'll get them next time…I promise…Lisa buries her face in Rodney's chest trying to regain her composure…I just want to go home Rodney…please just take me home.

Lisa is sitting in the kitchen staring down into her plate of scrambled eggs when her mom enters, its been two weeks since they got back and she hasn't heard from Rodney in over a week...why are you sitting here looking like somebody died...I'm good momma...just sitting

Babe, you ought to not take it too hard that it didn't work out, things happen when they are meant to happen.....Lisa looks up at her mother, I'm good momma....Lisa...tell me something...why didn't you ever try to make it work with that Michael....he was a nice boy and he really loved you...

Lisa gets up from the table and starts to leave the room...Michael...she exclaims...he was ok, but as far as loving me, the only thing he loved was that truck of his......Lisa says with a frown...

That truck is gone baby....he sold that truck. He sold it...Lisa exclaims...wow...that's hard to believe...

Not really...her mother says...the last thing I heard he went back to work for that silly David person......really......Lisa asks...how come you never mentioned that before...

Because you never asked me where I got the money for your trip......You think I had $4000.00 just laying around to give to you....Lisa stands motionless...staring over at her mother...yeah...he sold that truck so that you could go off to Vegas and be a big star....he asked me not to tell you....

Lisa backs away from the kitchen slowly, then turns and walks to her bedroom...as she enters, she closes the door behind her...then sits on the bed...all at once she feels a swell of emotion overtake her as she curls up into a ball...tears pouring from her eyes.

After a few minutes, Lisa gets up and goes to the window to close the curtains…as she reaches for the drawstring, she sees a black truck pull over across the street from her house, immediately she thinks of Michael and his promise to one day come for her, …after a brief pause she smiles a gentle smile as she watches a woman exit the truck…she's picking her child up from the daycare across the street…her heart rate begins to slow to normal……she turns her head to the right and sees a beautiful black Mercedes coming down the street, the car…its windows tinted, pulls behind the black truck across the street…Lisa stands frozen…there was a time when she imagined herself in a such a car…living the life she always pictured for herself…carefree….well off….

Lisa would've given anything to have that life at one time…now all she thought about was Michael….

The car door opens as a UPS truck moves slowly down the street obscuring her view…Lisa turns away from the window…then as if called by some unseen force, she turns again to see Michael walking across the street……a single rose in one hand….

Ebony Goddess.................hear my plea,

I've searched the world over, for one such as thee,

First time I saw you, just standing there,

Short skirt...braided doo...legs covered with hair,

My intent was to hit...then run was the plan,

Try you on, wear you out...send you home to your man,

But alas, as I watched you and I studied your groove,

I began to wonder...If I could love you,

If I could worship and care for, provide all that you need,

Cook your meals....buy your clothes, wash your hair...rub your feet,

If I could stand by your side, thru the good and the bad,

Buy a ring, then a home, plant my seed....be a dad!

If I could stay 50 years, while we age...no regrets,

Taking strolls thru the park, telling folks how we met,

All these things I could chance, and I would...just for you,

Wear this ring, take my name...share my love...

Say I Do

The End.....

63394927R00050

Made in the USA
Middletown, DE
01 February 2018